Tough times, good friends . . .

The ballerina stood on her toes, facing the man, her arms outstretched. When he was gone, the lights dimmed, and the ballerina was all alone in the blue spotlight. She bent her head sorrowfully and began a very slow, very sad solo dance.

Emma watched the ballerina and felt tears welling in her eyes. She sensed the woman's sadness as if it were her own. The woman was lonely.

A hot tear rolled down Emma's cheek. She understood how the ballerina felt. Emma felt abandoned by two people she adored and admired—her father and her friend Kerry. It was like she had lost a father and a sister all in one day.

An awful feeling made Emma's chest heave with a small sob. She felt all alone, as if she were invisible and there was no one in the world who could see her. Completely and terrifyingly alone.

Then she felt a warm hand on the back of her neck. . . .

Other books in the **NO WAY BALLET** series:

#1: Stepping Out
#2: A Twist of Fate

EMMA'S TURN

Suzanne Weyn

Illustrated by Joel Iskowitz

Troll Associates

Library of Congress Cataloging-in-Publication Data

Weyn, Suzanne.
Emma's turn / by Suzanne Weyn; illustrated by Joel Iskowitz.
p. cm.—(No way ballet ; #3)
Summary: Eleven-year-old Emma slights her new friends in the suburbs because she is excited about seeing her recently divorced father during her ballet class's field trip to Manhattan to see "The Nutcracker," but several disappointments help her put her new life in a better perspective.
ISBN 0-8167-1623-4 (lib. bdg.) ISBN 0-8167-1624-2 (pbk.)
[1. Friendship—Fiction. 2. Ballet—Fiction. 3. New York (N.Y.)—Fiction. 4. Divorce—Fiction.] I. Iskowitz, Joel, ill.
II. Title. III. Series: Weyn, Suzanne. No way ballet ; #3.
PZ7.W539Em 1990
[Fic]—dc19 89-31348

A TROLL BOOK, published by Troll Associates, Mahwah, NJ 07430

Printed in the United States of America.

10 9 8 7 6 5 4 3 2 1

Chapter One

This was the part of ballet class Emma hated the most. The girls gathered in one corner of the studio and, one by one, danced across the room imitating the series of steps their teacher, Miss Claudine, had just taught them.

"Please go ahead of me," Emma turned and whispered to the petite redhead behind her. "I'll be your best friend forever."

Charlie Clark shook her head no. "You're already my best friend. One of them, anyway. You'll have to do better than that, Emma Guthrie."

Emma thought a moment, readjusting the clip that held back her long brown hair. "I'll give you my new lipstick. Fuchsia pink," she offered, pursing her lips for Charlie to admire the color.

Charlie shook her head again. "My mother wouldn't let me wear it. She says ten is too young to wear makeup. Besides, fuchsia pink would look *horrendous* on me."

Horrendous was the girls' new favorite word. Last month it had been *humongous,* but they'd grown bored with it and switched to *horrendous.*

Charlie's eyes grew serious as she jerked her head toward the center of the studio. Emma followed Charlie's gaze and saw that their friend Lindsey Munson was in the middle of the room, wearing a tortured expression as she went through the ballet steps.

"No, no, Mademoiselle Lindsey," Miss Claudine called out patiently. "Stand up straight. Don't hunch over as if you were running for a goal on a football field. Hold your head high and slow down. Let the movements flow."

Lindsey gave the teacher a pained smile and tossed back her curly blond head in an effort to appear as straight-backed as Miss Claudine. Her square, athletic frame lost its usual energy and went limp. Her movements became extremely slow, as if she were walking underwater. She turned and did a slow, wobbly arabesque with her hands beating the air and her back leg jiggling behind her. Then she did a quick kick in front and took two extremely large steps toward the far side of the room.

"That was pretty horrendous," Emma whispered to Charlie.

"Wait till you see me," Charlie answered glumly.

"You? You're not worse than me!" Emma moaned.

Miss Claudine watched Lindsey finish the routine and sighed deeply. "Better, mademoiselle. You're getting there." She squinted her eyes and ran a long, delicate hand over her head to smooth her ash-blond hair, which was pulled back in a tight braid.

Emma, Charlie, and Lindsey all recognized the gesture. Miss Claudine always smoothed her hair when she was trying to think of a way to explain something to a student who was just not catching on. It was usually one of them. The three friends had the misfortune of being the worst beginning ballet dancers in Miss Claudine's School of Ballet.

Emma watched the girl ahead of her move gracefully through the routine. When her turn came, she took a deep breath and stepped out toward the middle of the floor.

"Remember your turnout," Miss Claudine coached. Emma pointed her toe and swiveled her leg out from the hip. Then her mind went blank. She couldn't remember any of the steps. Hoping to fake it, she smiled brightly and hopped across the room, flinging her legs out and spinning occasionally in a made-up performance of jumbled, imperfect ballet steps.

Miss Claudine rolled her blue eyes as the class giggled. "Very amusing, Mademoiselle Emma. Now, to the back of the line, and watch the other girls. See if you can't pick up the steps. Perhaps you'd like Danielle to go over them with you?"

"No, no," Emma replied quickly, casting a glance at dark-haired Danielle, who stood against the far wall smiling smugly back at her. The last thing she wanted was to have Danielle Sainte-Marie talking to her in her superior tone of voice. Danielle, who was slightly older and a much better dancer, was actually in the next class, intermediate ballet, but she came early to help Miss Claudine. "I'll get it next time," Emma assured her teacher.

Keeping in mind the threat of being "helped" by Danielle, Emma went to the end of the line and watched closely as a few more girls went through the routine. She saw Charlie stumble gracelessly across the room, and once again Miss Claudine squinted her eyes and smoothed back her hair.

When Emma's second turn came, she was pretty sure she had memorized the order of the steps. *Step, step, turn, turn, arabesque, kick, kick, step, step . . .* she silently repeated to herself as she moved across the room.

She was concentrating so hard that she was startled to see her own image as she reached the full mirror that covered an entire wall of the studio. She hardly recognized the intensity of the dark eyes staring back at her from beneath her delicately arched brows. Emma was suddenly self-conscious and stumbled a little. She twirled a stray piece of hair around her finger and faced Miss Claudine.

"Very good! It's amazing what the mademoiselle can do when she chooses to," Miss Claudine said, nodding her head approvingly.

This wasn't the first time Miss Claudine had hinted that Emma's only problem with ballet was that most of the time, she simply wasn't trying. "The body is flexible, but the mind is rigid," she'd observed of Emma one time during barre work. Miss Claudine had knelt, adjusting the position of Emma's legs as she continued to speak. "I know you have the ability, but I sense there is something in your head that doesn't want to learn. Overcome that, and someday you might be a very fine dancer."

Emma had been speechless, but Miss Claudine didn't seem to expect a reply. Emma had thought about Miss Claudine's words many times since then. She'd always insisted that she didn't like ballet because she wasn't good at it. But maybe she wasn't good at it because she didn't want to be. And she had a perfect excuse for that—her mother kept forcing her to take ballet class. Emma didn't like being forced or expected to do anything. "I want to be a painter," she always insisted, "not a ballet dancer."

Still, she liked this class more than any other class she'd managed to get herself kicked out of, and that was because she liked Miss Claudine. But, ballet was still a sore point with Emma.

"*Attendez,* class," Miss Claudine said, clapping her hands for attention. "There will be no story today because I wish to discuss something very important with you."

The class moaned. They all looked forward to the last part of class when Miss Claudine would tell them stories of different ballets. At those times, she was very dramatic, peppering the stories with the little French phrases she loved to use. Her eyes would well up with tears as she told the sad tale of the Swan Princess in *Swan Lake,* or she'd laugh aloud when she told the comic story of *A Midsummer Night's Dream.*

"Today I would like to discuss the possibility of a class trip with you. I have the chance to get a group rate on tickets to see a Sunday matinee of the great Christmas ballet, *The Nutcracker Suite,* at Lincoln Center."

The class murmured enthusiastically. "My parents

took me to see that when I was little," Emma told Lindsey and Charlie, who now sat cross-legged on the floor beside her.

"It was on TV last year, but I didn't watch it," said Lindsey, wiping the perspiration from her brow with the back of her hand. "I think there was something good on another channel, like *Wacky Sports Moments.*"

"I remember that," Charlie said. "It was a horrible night for TV. My parents wanted to watch *The Nutcracker,* my brothers all wanted to see that stupid sports thing, and I was dying to see a repeat of an episode of *The Forbingtons.* It was the one where Mimi gets remarried to Josh, and it was the only one I hadn't seen. So we all got in this horrendous fight, and my mother snapped off the TV and said fighting wasn't in the Christmas spirit. Then she actually made us all go out Christmas caroling. It was so—"

A soft cough made Charlie cut her story short. She looked up to see Miss Claudine staring at her. "Sorry, Miss Claudine," Charlie murmured, her face flushing.

Miss Claudine smiled her soft smile. "Thank you, mademoiselle. What I need to know from you, class, is if there are any dates when you cannot attend the performance. I would like you all to be able to come."

Lindsey looked at Charlie and Emma quickly, as if she were making up her mind about something. Then she raised her hand. "The week after Christmas isn't good for me, Miss Claudine," she said. "And I don't think it'll be good for Emma or Charlie."

Emma and Charlie looked at Lindsey with puzzled expressions.

"All right," said Miss Claudine. "Is there anyone else with a conflict?" Several other girls raised their hands and agreed that the week of winter break, right after Christmas, wasn't good for them, either.

"I could go after Christmas," Charlie said to Lindsey. "Why'd you tell Miss Claudine I couldn't?"

"I didn't want to tell you about this until I was sure," Lindsey whispered back. "My father is taking me to my cousins' house in the Adirondack Mountains for three days. He said I could bring a friend, but I've been trying to talk him into letting me bring *two* friends. I'm almost positive he'll say yes."

"That would be great!" Charlie cried, squeezing Lindsey's arm enthusiastically. "It would be so much fun. Wouldn't it be great, Emma?"

Emma drew her thin lips into a firm line. "It would be, but I don't think I could go, anyway," she replied seriously.

"You have to!" Charlie almost shouted. "Why not?"

Miss Claudine had been thumbing through a black date book. Now she looked up and was about to address the class again.

"I'll tell you after class," Emma whispered quickly.

"Is the Sunday before Christmas, the twentieth of December, good for everyone?" Miss Claudine asked. There was silence, and then a mumble of approval. "Very well, then," said the teacher, closing the date book. "The twentieth it is. The performance is at one, but we'll arrive by eleven-thirty, so I can show you around wonderful Lincoln Center." She then went on to tell them the price and to request permission slips. "*Au revoir, chéries,*" she said at last, dismissing the class in her usual manner.

"Why can't you come to the Adirondacks, Emma?" Lindsey asked in the dressing room after class. "We go skiing and skating, and sometimes we take walks in the woods. It's so pretty. And there's this big fireplace with a real old moose head over it."

"It sounds nice," said Emma, pulling her purple turtleneck sweater over her head, "but I'm going to spend winter break with my father in Manhattan."

"Maybe you could get out of it," Charlie suggested as she sat on the long bench and tied up the laces of her pink high-top sneakers.

"I don't want to get out of it," Emma replied, stuffing her leotard into her large tapestry bag and not meeting their eyes.

Charlie and Lindsey looked at one another. They always felt uncomfortable discussing Emma's parents' divorce. Emma only talked about it when the mood hit her, and that was rarely. They didn't feel right pressing her to say any more than she felt like saying, especially since they'd only known her a few months. Lots of the kids in school had divorced parents, and they seemed to survive just fine. Still, they knew Emma was sensitive about the subject.

"Guess what?" said Emma, suddenly brightening and looking up at them. "We're going to see *The Nutcracker* on my birthday. I'll be eleven on the twentieth."

"You didn't tell us your birthday was coming up!" cried Charlie.

"I just told you," Emma replied. "But it stinks having a birthday so close to Christmas. I just know I'd get twice as many presents if my birthday was in a different month. And sometimes my relatives send me one big present and say it's a combination birthday-Christmas gift. People are always forgetting your birthday, because they're all excited about Christmas."

"I'd hate it, too," Lindsey agreed. She was now dressed in faded jeans and a blue Yankees sweat shirt. She leaned against the wall, waiting for her friends, holding her blue down jacket in her arms. "Hey, Emma, don't forget to take off your makeup before your mother comes to pick us up," she reminded her friend.

"Thanks," Emma said, wiping her fuchsia pink lips with the back of her hand. Mrs. Guthrie insisted that ten was too young for a girl to wear makeup, but Emma was determined. She got around the problem by putting the makeup on after she left the house, and taking it off before she returned.

Emma stood before the small, frameless mirror on the wall and spit into a tissue, then wiped the blue eyeliner from her brown eyes. "My mother says I can wear some lip gloss and maybe mascara when I'm eleven," she told Charlie and Lindsey.

Danielle Sainte-Marie scurried into the dressing room. "What are you girls dawdling for?" she scolded. "The intermediate class has to get in here to change, you know."

"Why don't you stuff a sock in your mouth," Emma snapped.

"Why don't you act your age and not your shoe size," Danielle retorted.

When the older girl turned her back, Emma wrinkled her nose and stuck out her tongue. Charlie and Lindsey giggled, and Danielle whirled around to face Emma. The two girls glared at one another.

"Come on, your mother's waiting for us," Lindsey urged, breaking the tension. Danielle stormed out of the dressing room ahead of them.

The three girls walked slowly into the front room of Miss Claudine's. "Hey, catch this," Emma whispered. Charlie and Lindsey looked toward Miss Claudine's big desk and saw a very handsome man with wavy blond hair leaning against it, talking to Miss Claudine. He leaned even closer to say something to her in a low voice. Miss Claudine laughed prettily, looking into his eyes the whole time.

"I bet that's her boyfriend," Emma suggested eagerly.

"Maybe it's her brother," Lindsey said.

"No way," Emma disagreed. "Look at the way they're staring at each other. It's L-O-V-E."

Miss Claudine looked up suddenly, as if she sensed their eyes on her. Her lips formed a small smile. "Mesdemoiselles, I would like you to meet Adrian," she said. "We studied ballet together in Paris. We were the only two Americans in class. This is Mademoiselle Lindsey, Mademoiselle Emma, and Mademoiselle Charlotte."

"Charlie," Charlie corrected her teacher, hating the sound of her real name.

"It's a pleasure, ladies," Adrian said with a smile and a quick bow at the waist.

The girls smiled back at him. "See you Wednesday, Miss Claudine," said Charlie, waving as they left the front office and hurried out the glass door.

"He is *too* adorable," Charlie said excitedly once they were outside.

"And they met in Paris," Emma added. "That is the most romantic thing."

"I wonder if he's a dancer now," said Lindsey as they walked up the brightly lit corridors of the Eastbridge Mall toward the parking lot, where Mrs. Guthrie would be waiting for them in her sporty Jaguar.

"Why don't you two come to my house for lunch and we can figure it out," Emma suggested. The three friends loved guessing about Miss Claudine's life. Sometimes they made up wild stories. Other times they tried to piece together her life history from little clues she dropped. Miss Claudine was the most mysterious and unusual person they'd ever met. Wondering about her was one of their favorite pastimes. And now, here was a great, new, juicy clue.

The girls giggled about Adrian and stopped to look in the store windows as they made their way through the mall. Christmas carols played over a loudspeaker, and all the stores were decorated for the holidays. Santas were stationed every few yards, collecting toys and donations for the needy. They passed a fifteen-

foot decorated Christmas tree that stood in the middle of the mall.

Lindsey was suddenly seized with the Christmas spirit. A happy, grateful feeling warmed her. She put her arms around Emma and Charlie. "You guys are the best friends in the world," she said. Turning to Emma, she added, "I wish you could come on vacation with us."

Emma looked at her. "It would be fun, but I'm really looking forward to seeing my dad," she said, suddenly seeming very far away. "I miss him a lot."

Chapter Two

"This is the greatest TV set I've ever seen," said Charlie, gazing adoringly at the sleek, modern, wide-screen TV in Emma's living room. "I wish we had one like this."

"I've never met anyone who loved TV as much as you do," commented Lindsey as she sat gingerly on the edge of the white leather couch and paged through a large coffee-table book on the low glass table in front of her.

Charlie shrugged. "I know. It drives my mother crazy. She keeps calling me a couch potato, but I can't help it. I just love TV." Charlie turned from the set and looked around for a place to sit. "I can never get used to this furniture," she whispered. "It doesn't go with the outside of the house at all."

"I know, it's so . . ." Lindsey studied the large white leather couch with the two matching chairs on either side, the crimson-and-gold Oriental rug on the floor, and the brass-trimmed glass coffee table and matching end tables, trying to find the words to describe them. "It's all so . . . *nice.*"

"It's more than nice, though," said Charlie, seating herself on a black lacquer straight-backed chair with a white cushion. "This is city furniture. You can just tell it was bought for a city place."

"You're right," said Emma, coming into the room carrying a silver tray with their lunch on it. She set it down on the coffee table and passed out the tuna-fish sandwiches and glasses of milk. "My mother got all the furniture after the divorce. This is the same stuff we had when we lived on West Seventieth Street in New York."

"It's beautiful furniture," Charlie said quickly, hoping she hadn't offended Emma. "It's just not like the furniture in most other houses. This living room would be wrecked in one week in my house. I still can't believe your mother lets you eat in here."

"If she thought about it, she might not," said Emma, munching on her sandwich. "But in the city we always had a cleaning lady, and since we've come here, she's been so busy starting her literary agency that she doesn't have time to make a fuss about stuff like eating in the living room."

"You're lucky," said Charlie with her mouth full of tuna.

"What was it like living in the city?" Lindsey asked.

"It was the greatest. You could see all of Central Park from the terrace of our apartment," she said, her eyes sparkling with excitement as she remembered her old home. "And we had a doorman who always opened the door for you and got you a cab when you needed one."

"You took *cabs*?" exclaimed Charlie, obviously impressed.

"Yup. I took a cab to my old ballet school, once a week. It was on the East Side, and we lived on the West Side. When I was little, Rosa, my nanny, would go with me, but after a while I went by myself."

"How come you had a nanny?" asked Lindsey, wiping a milk mustache from her upper lip.

"Because both my parents worked. My dad's a lawyer, and my mother used to be an editor. Lots of kids in the city have nannies."

"I guess we just call them baby-sitters in Eastbridge," commented Charlie. " 'Nanny' sounds so old-fashioned."

"Well, we called them nannies," said Emma as she stretched out on the floor, leaning comfortably on her right elbow. "Wait until you see Lincoln Center. We lived real close to it. You won't believe the Metropolitan Opera House. It's got this giant chandelier in the lobby, and red carpet running all the way up the stairs. There are rows and rows of balconies. It's like being in a fairy-tale palace."

"What else is there?" asked Charlie.

"There are two other buildings—the New York State Theater and Avery Fisher Hall, but those are newer and plainer. The only one worth seeing is the Metropolitan. That's where I saw *The Nutcracker* when I was little, and I'm sure that's where we'll be going. I can't wait."

"Did you like living in the city better than Eastbridge?" asked Lindsey, realizing that she seldom saw Emma get so enthused about anything.

"Are you kidding?" Emma said. "Of course I did. There's no place like the city! I'm going back there as soon as I'm eighteen. I'm dying for winter break so I can go back." Suddenly Emma sat up straight. "I just had a great idea. Since I'll be in the city on my birthday, maybe I can get my father to take me out to brunch before the ballet. I'm going to call him right now."

"What's brunch?" asked Charlie.

Emma looked at her and shook her head. "I can't believe you don't know what brunch is. You people in the suburbs are so out of it sometimes."

"Excuse me," said Charlie, offended by Emma's tone. "I just never heard of it before, that's all."

"It's a combination of breakfast and lunch that you eat around noon or later. *Br,* breakfast. *Unch,* lunch. Get it?"

"I'd get too hungry," said Lindsey, neatly brushing crumbs off the coffee table and onto her plate.

"I'm going to go call my father," Emma excused herself. "I'll be right back."

She went to the kitchen and picked up the receiver of the white wall phone, then dialed her father's office. "Mr. Guthrie, extension four eleven, please," she said in her most businesslike voice to the receptionist on the other end of the phone.

Music played in Emma's ear as the receptionist put her on hold. Her expression lit up when her father's deep voice finally came over the phone. "Hi, Daddy. It's me."

"Hello, Emma. What's the matter, honey? Are you all right?"

Emma rolled her eyes. "I'm fine, Dad. Does something have to be wrong for me to call you?"

"Of course not. I'm glad you called. What's up?" Emma could picture him looking handsome in one of his beautiful suits, settling back in the large black leather swivel chair behind his big desk. He'd be holding the phone between his shoulder and chin, sorting through papers as he spoke. She'd seen him talk on the phone like that many times on her visits to his office.

"What are you doing on the twentieth?" she asked.

"The twentieth? Let me see, let me see. . . ." Emma could picture him flipping through the large alligator-skin datebook on his desk. "I'm checking. . . ."

"It's my birthday, Daddy!" Emma raised her voice in exasperation. "It's a Sunday."

There was a short silence on the other end, then her father chuckled. "I was teasing, Emma. Of course I knew it was your birthday. I have no plans."

"Good. Because my ballet class is taking a trip to Lincoln Center, and I thought I could meet you for brunch before the ballet."

"Will your mother be with you?" he asked in a tone that Emma thought was just a bit phony-casual.

"Nope. It will just be you and me," she answered.

"I'll have to juggle some other plans, but nothing's more important than my daughter's birthday. I'll meet you at Murphy's, right across the street from the Center. You remember where that is, don't you?"

"Of course I do, Daddy. We've only eaten there

about a million times. I'll meet you at Murphy's at a quarter to twelve."

"I'll look forward to it. We can talk about winter break then, okay?"

"Okay, bye."

"Bye, honey."

Emma hung up and ran back into the living room, smiling happily. "He's meeting me at Murphy's! We always used to eat there. It's the best restaurant in the world. I bet you he'll bring me a great birthday present, too. Miss Claudine won't mind, as long as my mother asks her if I can go."

"Boy, are you lucky," said Charlie.

"I just had another idea," Emma told them. "I'm going to call my best friend, Kerry. She lives right around the corner from where I used to live. Maybe she can get a ticket for the ballet that day."

"I thought we were your best friends," Lindsey said in a low, hurt voice.

"You are, absolutely," said Emma, stretching out on her stomach on the plush carpet. "You're my best Eastbridge friends. But Kerry and I have been friends since we were little. She's the coolest. She'll be thirteen in January, but she doesn't care that I'm younger. We used to do everything together. I can't wait to see her again."

"I guess Eastbridge friends aren't as good as city friends," said Charlie with a hint of anger in her voice.

"I didn't say that," Emma defended herself. "It's just that Kerry is so different from anyone you'd meet out here."

"I'm sorry we're so boring to you," Lindsey snapped, getting up from the couch.

"Well it *is* boring out here compared to living in the city," said Emma, annoyed. "I didn't say *you* were boring."

"You might as well have," Charlie replied.

"I can't believe what babies you guys are being," Emma said, climbing to her feet.

"Oh, now we're Eastbridge babies," said Charlie. "Sorry we can't all go around eating blunch all the time."

"Brunch," Emma corrected in an amused voice.

"Emma Guthrie, sometimes you can be the snobbiest girl in the world," said Charlie angrily. She turned and stormed toward Emma's front door.

"Where are you going?" Emma asked. "We didn't even get the chance to talk about Miss Claudine and Adrian."

"I'm walking home to my boring old house. What do you care?" Charlie shot back. "Call Kerry and talk to *her* about Miss Claudine."

"Can you believe her?" Emma asked Lindsey.

"Well, you make it seem like living in Eastbridge is torture or something," Lindsey answered. "And I'm sorry we're not as exciting as Kerry."

"Eastbridge *is* torture to me, and Kerry *is* different from anyone out here."

"Forget it, then. Charlie and I won't torture you with our boring selves anymore," Lindsey cried. She turned and headed for the door. "I'm coming with you," she called out to Charlie, who was already down the walkway.

Emma sat down on the couch as Lindsey let the door slam behind her. "Babies!" she grumbled to herself. "Big babies." She felt hot tears sting the edges of her eyes, but she was too angry to let them spill over. What right did they have to get so angry? She hadn't done anything wrong. What was so terrible about telling them about her life in the city?

Emma walked up the narrow stairs to her bedroom. The previous owners had added two attic dormers to the original house, and Emma used one of them as her bedroom. Her mother's bedroom was separated by a small bathroom and a staircase landing, so Emma had plenty of privacy.

She pushed her zebra-print comforter onto the floor and stretched out on her unmade bed. She sighed deeply and began picking at the purple polish on her fingernails.

Her mind wandered back to a time before her parents' divorce. She hadn't even realized there was anything wrong between them. They'd seemed happy to her, always going to the theater or out to dinner. They were good friends with the Hermans, Kerry's parents. The two couples often went out together, leaving Kerry and Emma together with Kerry's live-in nanny, Ruth.

What good times she and Kerry had had, Emma remembered. Ruth never paid much attention to them, and they'd been free to do what they wanted. One time Kerry had gotten hold of the freight-elevator key and they had spent the evening working the hand controls and riding up and down—even get-

ting stuck between floors for a while, not knowing whether to laugh or cry.

Then there was the time that Kerry found a way to climb into the central heating and cooling system. They'd climbed through the loosened grate and crawled into the wide ductwork. They were able to hear what people in every apartment on their floor were saying. They even spooked a whole cocktail party by making ghost sounds into the grate opening.

Emma missed Kerry, with her delicate freckled face and long, straight, whitish blond hair. Being friends with Kerry was like having the best big sister on earth—a sister who was always full of fun new ideas.

Her friendship with Kerry was just one of many things that had changed when Emma's mother moved them out here to Eastbridge. Emma had been in Eastbridge almost four months, and it just wasn't home to her. Becoming friends with Lindsey and Charlie was the best thing that had happened so far, but she still considered Kerry her closest friend. How could she compare friends she'd had for three months with one she'd had for years?

Emma hung her head down over the edge of the bed so she could see underneath. Fishing around among the shoes and books, she found her box of rainbow-colored stationery. She blew the dust off it. It was time to write Kerry a letter. She hadn't heard from her in two weeks.

"Dear Kerry," she wrote. "Hi, from your best friend, stuck out here in Boringsville." She went on to tell Kerry about Miss Claudine's trip to Lincoln

Center. " . . . So go to the box office and see if you can get a ticket for the ballet that day. Maybe I can talk my mother into letting me stay over at your place that night."

She wondered if she should tell Kerry about her fight with Charlie and Lindsey. No, she decided, it all sounded too babyish. Besides, Charlie and Lindsey would probably call her that night to apologize. She hoped so, anyway. She didn't want to go back to those first lonely days when she was new in Eastbridge.

What if they didn't call? Emma shook the unhappy thought from her head. They'd call.

"So, Kerry, let me know if you get the ticket," she concluded. "I'm dying, dying, *dying* to see you again."

Chapter Three

"This fight is dumb, and it's lasting too long," said Lindsey to Charlie as they stood shivering on the curb in the Eastbridge Mall parking lot with the rest of the ballet class.

"I never thought it would go this far," Charlie admitted. "But what are we supposed to do?"

It was the Sunday morning of their trip, and it was bitter cold. The girls were bundled up in their winter clothing, waiting for the two minibuses Miss Claudine had rented to come and pick them up.

"It's been almost two weeks, and Emma has hardly spoken to us," Lindsey continued, "except to make snobby remarks about Eastbridge."

"It's not our fault," Charlie argued. She could see her breath in the frosty air when she spoke. "I'm willing to forget about it. Emma's the one who's been walking around with her nose in the air. I don't think Eastbridge is heaven or anything, but she makes it sound like this is the dullest place on earth. She made me feel like we're just her friends until she can get back to the real fun people in New York."

Lindsey agreed. "That kind of hurt my feelings, too." She jogged in place to keep warm. "I can't believe my father made me wear this jumper on the coldest day of the year."

"You look nice," said Charlie, clapping her red-mittened hands together for warmth, glad she was wearing long wool pants.

"I hate dresses, and my legs are freezing in these tights," grumbled Lindsey, who only felt comfortable in jeans. "Here comes Emma now," she added, nodding toward the green Jaguar pulling into the parking lot.

"Today's her birthday, you know," Charlie reminded Lindsey.

"I know," said Lindsey. "I have her present, but I can't decide whether or not to give it to her."

"Me, too," Charlie said, pulling a small bundle wrapped in red tissue paper from the pocket of her long green coat. "I didn't figure this fight would last so long."

"Are you going to give her yours?" asked Lindsey.

"I can't decide, either," Charlie admitted. "I have to think about it some more. I'm still mad at her, and it doesn't feel right to give a present to someone you're angry at."

Charlie and Lindsey watched as Emma climbed out of the car. Emma always had a unique flair for dressing, favoring purple and black, but today she looked particularly distinct from the other girls. Her long brown hair hung straight and glistened at her shoulders, and she wore a purple beret tilted stylishly to one side. Over a black turtleneck sweater she had draped a purple poncho trimmed with a yellow-and-red Mexican design. Black tights and black ankle-high leather tie shoes completed the outfit.

"She's going to freeze with just that poncho on," commented Lindsey sensibly.

"She does look nice, though," Charlie replied.

Emma spotted her friends standing by the curb. For a moment she met their gaze, then all three girls turned away. Emma folded her arms tightly under her poncho. She was dying for this fight to be over. The last two weeks had been awful. During lunchtime she'd had to sit with girls she didn't really know, while Charlie and Lindsey sat together and shot icy glares her way. One day Charlie had offered her a potato chip from her bag, but Emma had been too proud to take it. She wasn't accepting a crummy old potato chip as a peace offering—not after the way they'd been acting. What she wanted was for them to apologize, and for the three of them to be best friends again, just like before.

Just then, two dark blue minibuses pulled into the parking lot and up to the curb. Miss Claudine stuck her head out of the window of the first one. *"Bonjour, chéries,"* she greeted them happily. She climbed out and slid open the side panel door. "You can ride in this bus or in the one behind, driven by Danielle's father, Monsieur Sainte-Marie."

Charlie and Lindsey looked quickly back at the other bus, and sure enough, there was Danielle, her brown hair set in abundant loopy curls. She sat proudly next to her balding father, who wore thick glasses, a plaid scarf, and the same self-satisfied expression as his daughter. He was behind the steering wheel smoking a pipe.

"I'm not sitting in there and smelling that horrendous pipe the whole way," stated Charlie. "Let's get into this bus, quick." They climbed into the warm bus in front of them and were excited to see that they recognized the driver. It was Adrian, Miss Claudine's handsome boyfriend.

"Wait until Emma sees this," whispered Lindsey excitedly, forgetting their feud for the moment. She looked around for Emma and saw her heading for the other bus, and then rapped loudly on the window to get her attention. As Emma looked up, Lindsey motioned her to come into their minibus.

Emma climbed aboard, taking a seat ahead of Charlie and Lindsey. "Thank you for the warning," she said primly. "I don't think I could have stood the ride in with The Saint and her father." Put off by Emma's stiff tone, Charlie and Lindsey remembered that they were in a fight and simply nodded politely back to her.

A thin girl named Tish was the last to climb in. She took the empty seat next to Emma. "Hi, Tish," Emma said in a voice that was just a little too loud. "I love your coat."

Tish looked down at her red wool coat. "Thanks," she said. "I like your poncho."

"Ready, ladies?" asked Adrian, turning around in the driver's seat. His lively dark eyes seemed to sparkle. "As soon as Claudine gets here, we'll be off."

In a few more minutes, Miss Claudine had taken her place beside Adrian, and they were heading through the parking lot and out of the mall. They rode in silence at first. When Miss Claudine pulled off her red beret the girls noticed she'd set her hair in soft curls that fell prettily around her shoulders. Under her coat they saw that she wore a solid red knit dress. Her sharp features seemed softer today, and the makeup she wore—mascara and red lipstick—made her blue eyes look especially bright.

"She looks so different," whispered Lindsey.

Charlie fluttered her eyes and dramatically placed a hand over her heart. "She's with her true love, that's why," she whispered back, and they both giggled.

Before long, the girls were all talking among themselves, and the bus was filled with a low buzz of chatter broken by occasional laughter. Charlie and Lindsey soon heard one voice rising above the others. It was Emma's.

"You don't know how happy I am to be going back to the city, Tish," she said. "All my friends are still there. It's where I really belong."

"I've only been to the city a few times," said Tish.

"That's a lot more than some people can say," replied Emma. "I suppose *some people* just can't understand city life. My very best friend Kerry lives in New York. She's the greatest. She did the most hysterical thing one time. . . ."

"That does it," said Charlie in a low growl as Emma chattered on about Kerry. "She is definitely not getting this birthday present."

Lindsey nodded. When she spoke, it was in a voice

even louder than Emma's. "We're going to have so much fun in the mountains, Charlie, just the two of us," she said. "I can't wait to ski on Whiteface Mountain. The skiing is wonderful, and they have the greatest lodge. We can take lessons if you want. They have the cutest ski instructors."

"It sounds great," said Charlie in an equally loud voice. "And I can't wait to meet your cousins. What are their names again?"

"Paul, Richard, and Mike. Paul's twelve, Richard's fourteen, and Mike's seventeen. They're the nicest guys. This year, Mike's going to rent a snowmobile. He can take us out for rides."

Emma cast a quick glance over her shoulder and raised her voice even louder. "I'll be meeting Kerry today. We've spent every one of my birthdays together for the last five years. She always gives me a gift that is so unusual. Last year she gave me a purple marble elephant that came all the way from India."

"And there's skating and sledding . . ." Lindsey shouted.

"Mesdemoiselles!" scolded Miss Claudine from the front seat. "Conversation is fine, but please lower your voices."

Emma shot a withering glance at Charlie and Lindsey, who glared right back at her. Emma turned around in her seat and gazed out the window. A big part of her wanted to make peace, but another part felt she was the one who deserved an apology. After all, Charlie and Lindsey had walked out in a huff. The last two weeks had been hard without them, but had just convinced Emma all the more that she didn't belong in Eastbridge.

In little over an hour they were heading down the Henry Hudson Parkway. Emma wrapped her arms around herself in anticipation. This was going to be a wonderful birthday. First brunch with her father, then the Metropolitan Opera House, and then the chance to see Kerry again. She decided to call home from the city and beg her mother to let her spend that night at Kerry's.

She took a quick peek over her shoulder at Lindsey and Charlie. They were staring out the windows at the tall buildings. In just three months she'd grown used to sharing everything with them. It hurt to have them sitting together without her. Still, her pride kept her sitting in her seat. It was her birthday, and they should be the ones to apologize to her. If they didn't say they were sorry, then she certainly wasn't going to.

Soon Adrian drove the bus down a ramp into the parking lot below Lincoln Center. He stopped in front of a glass booth, and an attendent gave him a receipt.

The bus driven by Mr. Sainte-Marie pulled in next. When everyone had gotten off the buses, Miss Claudine led the way up the ramp to Lincoln Center. They walked up low, wide steps, and past the fluttering flags and banners that lined the front of the majestic plaza.

"Wow!" said Charlie when she stood and faced the three large buildings, set in a U shape, that made up the Lincoln Center complex. "It's so big!"

Miss Claudine led them to the center of the plaza to the fountain spurting graceful arcs of water. "I will pick up any lost souls here at this fountain. If you find yourself lost, come to this spot. The complex is big and can be confusing, so please do not stray, *chéries.* It would be most inconvenient for the rest of us, and it would cause me great alarm." Miss Claudine spread her arms and smiled at them warmly. "To your left is the New York State Theater," she said, gesturing toward the large, square building with a long balcony. "That's where we will see today's performance."

"You mean it's not going to be at the Met?" questioned Emma, clearly disappointed.

"No, mademoiselle," Miss Claudine answered. "Have you ever been to this theater?" Emma shook her head. "It is a lovely, if more simple, theater," Miss Claudine told her. "I want each of you to hold on to your ticket," she continued, pulling a stack of orange tickets from her coat pocket and handing one to every girl.

Emma checked her purple plastic watch. It was 11:35. She looked over her shoulder. Murphy's was right across the street, the clean windows of its glassed-in porch sparkling in the late-morning light.

"Now we will start our tour of beautiful Lincoln Center," Miss Claudine announced. "You won't feel the cold so much when we are moving, and perhaps we can stop for hot chocolate before the ballet."

"Miss Claudine!" Emma called, raising her hand. "Can I be excused to go meet my father? Remember you told my mother it would be all right?"

"But of course, *chérie,*" said Miss Claudine. "Adrian, would you please escort the mademoiselle across the street to Murphy's?"

"It would be my pleasure," Adrian answered gallantly.

Charlie and Lindsey watched as Emma and Adrian made their way down the broad steps of Lincoln Center Plaza. "And here to your right is Avery Fisher Hall. . . ." Miss Claudine began her tour.

Chapter Four

Charlie and Lindsey stood in front of Avery Fisher Hall and watched Emma and Adrian cross the busy street. "Wouldn't you love to get a look at her father?" Charlie asked.

"I'm pretty curious," Lindsey agreed. "Emma makes him sound like he's perfect."

Lindsey and Charlie scrunched their faces into thoughtful expressions. "It's no use," said Lindsey after a moment. "I just can't think of a way we can get to see him."

"Me, neither," Charlie admitted. "But keep thinking about it."

The two girls followed the rest of the class as Miss Claudine guided them through Avery Fisher Hall, showed them where the orchestra played, and told them stories about the plaques and artwork in the lobby.

Adrian returned from Murphy's and brought up the rear of the group, along with Mr. Sainte-Marie.

"We could ask Adrian what Emma's father looks like," Lindsey suggested.

"Nah," Charlie said. "Wouldn't you feel dumb? And besides, it wouldn't be the same as seeing him for ourselves."

"You're right," Lindsey decided.

The group left Avery Fisher Hall and followed Miss Claudine to the front of the Metropolitan Opera House. It was closed, but Miss Claudine told them about the many great opera and ballet stars who had performed there.

"You will see the State Theater for yourselves," she concluded. A shiver of cold made her shoulders shake. "Now let's cross the street and get some hot cocoa," she said with a smile. "I think we could all use some."

She led them down the stairs and across the street to a small coffee shop just a few buildings away from Murphy's. Some of the girls piled into booths while others swiveled on the stools at the counter.

Charlie and Lindsey perched on stools, still trying to come up with a way to catch a glimpse of the mysterious Mr. Guthrie. Miss Claudine ordered them all cups of hot chocolate. Pulling off their gloves, they let the steam from the hot drink waft up and thaw their frozen faces.

Charlie sniffed and reached into her jacket pocket for a tissue to wipe her runny nose. She pulled out a crumpled white tissue and her wallet, and she stared at the wallet thoughtfully.

"What is it?" Lindsey asked.

"I just might have an idea," Charlie told her. She

leaned into the aisle and found Miss Claudine checking the booths to make sure all the girls had received their hot chocolate.

"Miss Claudine? Miss Claudine," Charlie called.

The teacher looked over at her. "Yes, *chérie,* what is it?"

"I forgot that Emma asked me to hold her wallet," Charlie lied, waving the wallet at her teacher. "I think she's going to need it. Can Lindsey and I go give it to her in the restaurant?"

Miss Claudine frowned. "Why not give it to her when she returns?"

Charlie was stumped, but Lindsey came to her rescue. "There are some pictures in here that she was dying to show her father. She's going to be *so* disappointed if he doesn't get to see them."

"All right," Miss Claudine agreed, slowly nodding her head. "Murphy's is just two buildings down."

"We know," Charlie chirped happily, hopping off her stool.

"Come directly back," Miss Claudine warned.

"Oh, we will," Lindsey assured her.

Miss Claudine followed them to the front door and watched as they turned the corner to enter Murphy's. They looked back and waved to her as they disappeared from her sight.

"We can't let Emma see us," said Lindsey.

"We'll just stick our heads in and then leave," Charlie agreed. "I just want to get a look at this mystery dad."

They stepped into the revolving door and pushed it around to the inside of the restaurant. They were met immediately by the maître d'. "Can I help you, ladies?" he asked suspiciously.

The girls gazed up sheepishly at the tall, thin, balding man wearing a charcoal gray suit and a white flower in his lapel. "We're waiting for our father," Charlie spoke up. "We're meeting him here for blunch."

The man raised an eyebrow at them skeptically. "She means brunch," Lindsey explained quickly.

"I see," the maître d' replied stiffly. He stepped over to a large notebook on a podium. Lindsey stood on her toes and saw that the page was marked *Reservations* at the top. "And what is your father's name?"

"Munson . . ."

"Clark . . ." the girls answered at once.

The maître d' coughed lightly and looked at Charlie and Lindsey impatiently. "Northrop Munson-Clark the Third," Charlie told him, trying to sound as snooty as the wealthy Alicia Koop-Forbington from her favorite television show, *The Forbingtons.*

Lindsey's mouth curved into a smile, but she controlled it. "Surely you've heard of Daddy," she added.

The man sighed and ran a long finger down the reservations list. "I don't see Mr. Munson-Clark's reservation," he said.

"Don't tell me Daddy forgot!" wailed Charlie.

"Now, now." Lindsey patted Charlie's shoulder. "We'll just wait for Daddy right here. You don't mind, do you, sir?"

The man looked as if he did mind very much. "Oh,

just sit right there," he grumbled, motioning toward a wooden bench.

"We've got to get back," Lindsey whispered nervously.

"Just another five minutes," Charlie replied in a low voice. "We've gotten this far."

They sat on the bench with their hands folded in their laps, smiling sweetly at the maître d' every time he cast a doubtful glance their way. After a few minutes, they began to feel overheated and wiggled out of their coats, folding them carefully on their laps.

Finally, a lady in a mink coat and a man in a tan overcoat came through the revolving door. The maître d' grabbed two menus and, exuding a charm he hadn't bothered to waste on Charlie and Lindsey, ushered the couple into the dining room.

The minute the maître d' was out of sight, the girls hurried into the barroom across from the podium, clutching their coats. The bar was separated from the dining room by a solid mahogany wood partition that rose four feet from the floor.

Except for the bartender, who was reading the Sunday *Times* at the far end of the bar, the room was empty. Lindsey and Charlie crouched low and scurried to hide behind an empty table next to the partition. They knelt down until they were sure no one had seen them, then they cautiously peered over the partition into the dining room.

"There she is!" Charlie pointed to Emma, who was seated across from a man and a woman at one of the dining room tables. "She doesn't look too happy, either."

The man was everything Charlie and Lindsey had

imagined when Emma spoke of her father. He was tall and handsome, with a full head of wavy black hair, and he wore a soft-looking tan sweater under a tweed jacket. The pretty woman with him had long, yellow-blond hair held back by a large black velvet bow. She was wearing a black pantsuit and a white ruffled blouse.

Mr. Guthrie appeared to be doing all the talking, and the blond woman beside him nodded and laughed at everything he said. Emma was the only one who didn't seem to be enjoying herself. Her shoulders were slumped, and when she lifted her head occasionally, it was only to scowl darkly at the woman.

"Who do you think she is?" asked Lindsey, looking at Charlie with a puzzled expression.

"That's got to be Mr. Guthrie's girlfriend," Charlie said seriously.

"No!" Lindsey gasped. "You don't know that. Maybe she's a relative."

Charlie shook her head. "Look at Emma," she pointed out. "That's a stare of pure hatred she's giving that woman. Did you ever glare at a relative with that kind of drop-dead expression?"

Lindsey considered a moment. "No. I never even looked at my Aunt Mariel like that—and she's the most annoying relative I have."

"Exactly," Charlie said confidently.

They watched a little longer as a waiter in a large tan apron brought out their meal. "Blunch just looks like plain old breakfast to me," whispered Charlie.

"Emma looks like it's about to make her sick,"

Lindsey commented, watching Emma push the food around on her plate.

Charlie was about to answer, but suddenly she sensed a presence behind them. She turned and gazed up at the maître d', who stood staring down at the two girls, his arms folded tightly across his chest. "Searching for Daddy?" he asked sarcastically.

Lindsey and Charlie jumped up guiltily. "Uh . . . yes," said Lindsey. "Daddy sometimes forgets he's meeting us and goes right in. He's very absent-minded."

"He's a problem, really," Charlie added. "He's always been a little . . . you know." She twirled her finger near her right temple to indicate that "Daddy" was a little flaky.

"Children are not allowed in the restaurant unescorted," the man informed them coldly. "Please confine yourselves to the front waiting room."

"Sure thing," Lindsey said as she and Charlie grabbed up their coats and walked back to the front room. "In fact, we were going to leave anyway." Lindsey and Charlie slipped hurriedly into their coats.

"Yes, and if Daddy comes, tell him we're ever so annoyed," said Charlie in her Alicia Koop-Forbington voice. "We may never speak to him again." With that, Lindsey and Charlie stuck their noses up in the air and spun through the revolving door to the frosty outdoors.

"It feels even colder now," complained Charlie, zipping up her coat. "Boy, what a grouch that guy was."

"I know," Lindsey agreed, pulling on her black wool gloves. They turned the corner and saw Miss Claudine leading the class directly toward them.

She looked at them with sharp eyes. "Mesdemoiselles, where have you been?" she asked, a rare note of anger in her warm voice. "You were supposed to return directly. I was coming to get you."

"Umm . . . uh . . ." Lindsey stammered.

"We had a little trouble finding Emma at first," said Charlie. That was partly true, anyway.

"Monsieur Guthrie is supposed to bring Emma to the theater. Is that still the plan?" Miss Claudine asked.

Emma and Charlie shrugged. "I guess so," said Charlie.

"Very well, then, we will go back without her." Miss Claudine clapped her hands and instructed the class to be careful and stay together when they crossed the busy street in front of Lincoln Center.

Adrian came up behind Lindsey and Charlie as they got to the back of the group. "Did you girls get stuck in the revolving door?" he asked pleasantly.

"No," Charlie answered with a smile, relieved that he was making light of the fact that they'd been gone so long. If Miss Claudine were very upset with them, he probably wouldn't have made a joke.

"I hope Emma makes it back in time," said Lindsey to Charlie. "Do you think she will?"

"Who knows?" Charlie replied. "Maybe she'll poison that woman's lunch and the police will take her away."

Lindsey twisted her face at Charlie. "You definitely watch too much TV," she said.

"Maybe," admitted Charlie, "but I've never seen Emma look so angry before."

Chapter Five

Mr. Guthrie pushed his chair back from the table and stretched his arms behind him. "Well, that was delicious, as usual. How were your eggs Benedict, Dawn?"

"Just scrumptious, Mark," answered the blond woman beside him.

"My mother says their eggs Benedict taste like rubber covered with wallpaper glue," said Emma. "She says no one in their right mind would eat the eggs Benedict here."

"I never heard her say that, Emma," her father said, a distinct note of irritation in his deep voice.

"Everyone has their own taste," Dawn replied. "I liked the eggs very much."

"I'm just telling you what Mom said," Emma told them with a shrug of her shoulders. "It's no big deal."

"How would you like some of Murphy's famous strawberry shortcake for dessert, Emma?" her father asked. "I know you love it."

"I don't have time, Dad," Emma answered. Normally she adored Murphy's desserts, but meeting Dawn had altogether destroyed her appetite. How could her father actually be dating this human Barbie doll! How could he be dating anyone?

Of course, Emma knew that he was divorced and technically he was allowed to date, but the idea of it made Emma sick to her stomach. She knew lots of kids whose parents were divorced and dated, and who'd even married other people. It didn't seem like a big deal when it happened to them. Now that it was happening to her, though, it was a different story.

"Okay then, let's talk about winter break before you go," her father said. Emma didn't like the serious look on his face. It was an expression he wore when he didn't have good news to tell. "I have some bad news. I'm afraid I have to be out of town until the thirtieth."

Emma counted on her fingers under the table. "But that leaves us only three days, Daddy. I have to be back at school on Monday the fourth, and Mom wants me to come home that Sunday. Can't you get out of it?"

"I'm sorry," he answered. "I have to see a very important client in Colorado. It's simply too late to do anything about it."

Emma looked down at the half-eaten food on her plate. "I was really looking forward to it," she mumbled, not meeting her father's gaze. "I've been looking forward to it ever since we moved."

"There's good news, though," said her father with a cheeriness which seemed somewhat forced to

Emma. "When I get back, we are going to have the best three days you can imagine. Dawn has planned everything. She got tickets to a Broadway play and made reservations at the best restaurants in town. The three of us are going to have a ball!"

Emma looked at Dawn. There was nothing truly horrendous about her, Emma thought—if you liked bland, boring people. But she certainly didn't want to spend her winter break with Dawn. That was supposed to be *her* time with her father.

"That reminds me," her father went on, pulling a box wrapped in silver paper and tied with a red satin bow out from behind his chair. "Happy birthday!"

Emma smiled for the first time that day. "Thanks, Daddy." She tore at the paper and lifted the lid off the large box. Her smile stayed frozen on her face, but her eyes lost their brightness when she looked down in the box and saw a powder blue jogging suit with pink cuffs.

"If it's not the right size, I can change it," Dawn offered.

"I know you love purple, but Dawn convinced me that blue is a much more flattering color for a girl your age," her father added.

Emma was speechless. What had her father been thinking? He knew she hated sports—she would never wear this suit to go jogging. And she'd rather die than wear anything in powder blue. This present was picked out by someone who didn't know her at all. Someone like . . . Dawn.

"It's fine," Emma mumbled. "Thank you." She shut the box quickly and pushed it aside. "I'd really better go now, or I'll be late," she said, feeling the tingle of tears rising again.

"Let me get the check and we'll walk you over to Lincoln Center," her father said.

"No, really, Daddy, it's okay," Emma told him, pushing back her chair. All she wanted was to get out of there, away from him, Dawn, and the powder blue jogging suit. "I didn't realize how late it was. I'm meeting Kerry." She kissed him quickly on the cheek and then hurried out of the dining room.

"You forgot your present," she heard him call, but she didn't turn around. She didn't want him to see the tears that now ran down her face.

"Can I get the young lady her coat?" asked the maître d'.

"Yes, please," Emma answered, turning her face away to hide her tears. "It's the poncho and purple beret."

The man handed Emma her poncho and hat. The sight of the poncho made her tears flow even more freely. It had been one of the presents her parents gave her for her birthday last year. She loved it, and she'd insisted on wearing it today, even though her mother had said it wasn't warm enough. She wanted her father to see how much the gift meant to her.

Emma hurried through the revolving door. She quickly wiped away her tears and put her beret on her head. Some horrendous birthday brunch this had turned out to be, she thought miserably.

She knew it had to be close to one, so she bent her head against the wind and headed back to Lincoln Center. At least Kerry would be there. Kerry would understand how inconsiderate her father had been. She'd make fun of Dawn, and soon they'd both be laughing. Kerry would make her feel better.

The wind whipped through the small trees on the sidewalk. Emma saw a woman chase her gray felt hat down the street as the breeze carried it along. She crossed her arms under her poncho to keep warm. It was definitely getting colder. There was now a good-sized crowd of people in the plaza. Some hurried by, others stood around waiting. As Emma walked up the steps, she searched the crowd for Kerry. She'd arranged to meet her friend at the fountain, but when Emma got there, Kerry hadn't arrived yet.

She looked toward the State Theater. The class had probably gone in, but since Miss Claudine had already given out the tickets, Emma knew she could still find her seat. *Hurry up, Kerry,* she thought, jiggling up and down for warmth. *It's freezing out here!*

At that moment, someone behind Emma grabbed her shoulders. "Boo!" said a familiar voice.

Emma whirled around to face a pretty girl wearing a short blue coat over a short denim skirt. Her long blond hair was pushed back with a furry red headband. "Kerry!" Emma cried, hugging her friend happily.

"You look great, kiddo," said Kerry. "Not wearing much makeup anymore, I see."

"I met my father for brunch, and he hates it when I wear makeup. Now that I'm eleven, my mother said lip-gloss and mascara were okay, so that's all I wore."

"You're eleven now?" Kerry asked.

"My birthday is today," Emma told her slowly, hurt that Kerry had forgotten.

"Gee, it slipped my mind," Kerry said with a mischievous smile. "Boy, I feel terrible."

"You don't look like you feel terrible," Emma said in a sulky tone.

"That's because I didn't forget, dodo-head," said Kerry. She dug into her bag and pulled out a gift wrapped in yellow-and-blue-striped paper. "Happy birthday!"

Emma smiled and hugged Kerry again. She ripped open the paper. "I can't wait to open this," she said. "You always get me the best presents!" Inside was a slim hardcover book. *"The River of Inward Being: The Poems of Harley Fencer,"* Emma read off the cover. "I didn't know you liked poetry, Kerry. Is it good?"

"The best," said Kerry, her eyes glowing. "It's Ian's favorite book, and he suggested I get it for you."

"Ian?" Emma asked, puzzled.

Kerry leaned in close. "Ian Brentwood and I are going together. It's been two weeks. Here he comes now." Emma looked to where Kerry pointed and saw a tall boy of about fifteen in a black overcoat with chin-length blond hair walking toward them.

"Hello," he greeted Emma. "I see you've opened your copy of *The River.* You'll love it. It changed my life."

"It did?" Emma asked. "How?"

"I came to realize that it's foolish to attempt anything. The river of life will carry you wherever you need to be."

"Tell that to my mother when I have to do my math homework," Emma laughed. Ian nodded seriously, not getting the joke. "Listen, we'd better go inside," Emma told them, noticing that there was no one left in front of the theater.

Kerry took Emma's elbow and walked her a few steps away from Ian. "Emma, I need a best-friend favor," she said in a low, intimate voice. "My parents don't like Ian—they don't want him in our apartment. So I never get to see him. I told my parents I'd be with you, but would you mind if I sold my ticket and spent the day with him, instead? Ian and I just never get to spend enough time together."

Emma couldn't believe her ears. "You don't get to spend *any* time with me," she said.

"Don't be a baby, Emma," Kerry said. "This is different. And I'll get to see you all through winter break."

Emma wanted to tell Kerry about how Dawn had messed up her entire winter break, but the word *baby* was still ringing in her ears. Because she was two years younger than Kerry, it had always been important to Emma that Kerry not think of her as immature. Emma knew that by calling her a baby Kerry had always gotten Emma to do things her way. She knew it was a maneuver on Kerry's part, but it was a maneuver that worked.

"Sure, go ahead. I understand," she said. "I don't know how we'll sell your ticket, though. Everyone's inside already."

"Ian will sell it," Kerry explained. "I knew you'd agree. What are best friends for?"

"Right," Emma agreed halfheartedly.

Kerry planted a kiss on Emma's cheek. "Thanks for being such a pal," she said. "You'll really like getting to know Ian during your break. He's the most sensitive boy I've ever met."

"Yeah, I can't wait."

Kerry grabbed Ian's hand happily. "See you in a week or so," she said, waving to Emma as she began walking away. "And happy birthday again."

Emma waved back and watched Kerry run down the steps with Ian. She saw him stop a man and sell the ticket. Emma opened the book of poetry to the middle. She read a short poem out loud. " 'Flea. The flea and me. What is flea? Without me.' " She rolled her eyes and snapped the book shut. *I'll just leave this here for some sensitive poetry lover to find,* she said to herself as she laid the book down on the ground.

She began walking toward the State Theater. All her wonderful birthday plans had fallen apart. Brunch had been horrible. Kerry would rather spend the day with Ian. And the ballet wasn't even in the Metropolitan Opera House. She looked over at the grand, glass-fronted building that stood dark and quiet at the far end of Lincoln Center. Everything that was magical to Emma about Lincoln Center, about all of Manhattan, was represented by the opera house. She stared at the graceful white columns that arched around the many panes of glass. It was so beautiful.

And I'm not even going to get to see it, she thought darkly. She looked at the modern State Theater with its clean, sensible lines, and then back to the opera house, its glass shimmering in the afternoon light. "Oh, yes I *am* going to see it," Emma said to herself, and abruptly changed direction.

Chapter Six

"Hey, look, Kerry left with her geeky boyfriend," said Charlie, her nose almost pressed up against the glass door of the State Theater.

"I thought she was going to see the ballet with Emma," said Lindsey.

"I did, too, but she left." Lindsey and Charlie had been watching Emma from inside the theater ever since they spotted her standing by the fountain.

"*Attendez, mesdemoiselles,*" said Miss Claudine. "We will be going in now. Have your tickets ready." The class lined up behind their teacher.

"We'd better get in line," Lindsey said. "Is Emma coming?"

"She put that book down and she's walking this way," Charlie answered. "She looks really sad. It's hard to stay mad at anyone who's having such a crummy birthday."

"I know," Lindsey agreed. "Let's get in line. We don't want her to know we've been spying on her."

Lindsey took a place at the end of the line, but Charlie lingered at the door.

Suddenly Charlie looked over at Lindsey with a surprised expression. "Come here," she called to Lindsey. "Look at this."

Lindsey rejoined Charlie, and the two girls watched as Emma walked away from the theater. "Where could she be going now?" Charlie wondered aloud.

"I don't know, but I think we should go after her," Lindsey said. "She looked kind of upset."

"But we're having a fight, remember?" Charlie protested.

"Yeah, but it's a stupid fight," said Lindsey. "You know we're going to make up sooner or later. And I just have this feeling Emma needs some friends right now."

"Miss Claudine will kill us if she notices we're gone."

"I know," Lindsey replied seriously. "The performance is about to start, though. Maybe she won't realize we're gone until intermission. We've just got to help Emma."

"Okay, you're right," Charlie gave in. "Let's go." With a brief check over their shoulders, they saw that Miss Claudine was waiting for her students on the other side of the ticket taker. For the moment, she was busy talking to Adrian.

They slipped quickly out the door and spotted Emma in front of the Metropolitan Opera House talking to a security guard. The guard had opened the door a crack, and Emma was waving her arms wildly in the air as she spoke.

"What is she up to?" Lindsey asked as they ran toward the theater.

"Knowing Emma, it could be anything," said Charlie, who knew from past experience that when Emma set her mind to something, nothing stopped her. "Look! The guard is letting her in."

The girls slowed to a trot and watched as Emma disappeared inside the great dark building. "Now what?" asked Lindsey when they reached the front of the Opera House.

"If Emma got in, then so can we," said Charlie, cupping her hands around her eyes and peering through the glass into the theater lobby. She spotted the security guard sitting at a small table watching a portable TV. She rapped hard on the glass for his attention. He looked up and then slowly ambled toward them, opening the door with a key from a large ring.

"Are you looking for the kid whose mother works here as a cleaning lady?" he asked, sticking his head out the door.

Charlie and Lindsey looked at one another, then back at the guard. "No," said Charlie. "We have to talk to our friend who you just let in."

"That's the same kid. She had to give her mother an urgent message. Something about her cousin from Poland arriving unexpectedly and going into labor in their living room. I don't know, I couldn't get it straight."

"That's her," Lindsey said. "Can we come in? We have something important to tell her."

"Her cousin had a girl," Charlie added.

"That's nice," said the guard. "But you'll have to wait out here. I shouldn't have even let her in. She was just so frantic that I felt sorry for her."

"But we—" Lindsey began to protest. It was no use. The guard ended the discussion by closing the door and locking it behind him.

"I guess we'll just have to wait," said Charlie, leaning up against one of the large freestanding signs outside the opera house. The sign showed a sleek ballerina in a knee-length gauze ballet dress looking regal as she stood high on her toes, one leg poised delicately in the air. Her eyes shone as she gazed at her tall, handsome ballet partner. "Don't they look perfect?" said Charlie, stepping back to admire the sign.

"The Jacques Roman Opera Ballet Troupe," Lindsey read. "Performing with the Jacques Roman Opera." Lindsey, who never considered herself graceful in any way, stood and admired the flowing lines of the ballerina's pose. "She's really beautiful," she said, her voice filled with awe. "She's like a princess."

"Her partner isn't bad, either," Charlie pointed out, tapping the picture of the man who looked so self-assured in a red military jacket and black tights. "The sign says they'll be dancing here next week. I wonder if they look as good in person."

The girls studied the poster for a few more minutes as they waited for Emma to come out. "We can't wait forever," Lindsey commented after a while. "I guess we might as well go back and see *The Nutcracker.*"

COMING
NEXT WEEK!
Jacques
Roman
OPERA BALLET CO
JULIA AND ADAM INC.

"Emma's going to be in trouble if she doesn't get back soon," said Charlie with a worried expression.

"I know, but what can we do?"

"If only there was another way into this theater," Charlie mused. Just then, they saw two men and three women walking toward them from across the plaza. All of them were young, in their late teens or early twenties, and they carried large dance bags.

"They're dancers," Charlie said.

"How can you tell?"

"Look at their ankles," she said, pointing to the heavy, brightly colored warm-up socks all of them wore. "And those bags probably have their ballet stuff in them," Charlie continued. "Just look at the way they walk—so straight."

The group passed close by Charlie and Lindsey, and the girls could hear them chattering happily in another language. "That sounds like French to me," said Lindsey. "I bet you're right. Maybe they're going inside for a rehearsal."

Charlie and Lindsey had the same thought at the same time. Without a word, they followed the group of dancers, keeping just a few yards behind them at all times. The dancers turned the corner of the opera house and headed toward the back of it. They stopped in front of the stage door and waited as one of the women fished a key from her pocket. When she'd opened the door, the others filed in behind her. The last one in let the door close slowly on its own.

"Hurry up," cried Lindsey. She sprinted to the door and grabbed the metal handle just as it was almost completely shut. Smiling back at Charlie, she waited for her to catch up. Then, carefully, they cracked the heavy door open.

It took a minute for their eyes to adjust to the darkness, but they quickly realized that they were looking backstage. They heard voices coming from the stage farther in, but no one was standing near the door. Silently, they pulled the door open wider and crept inside.

"Wow! It's so big it makes me feel like a mouse," whispered Charlie, staring up at the high ceilings.

They stood against the wall in the darkness and watched as people hurried about. One tall man in a red plaid shirt and jeans passed them, shouting, "I'm going to need a spotlight centerstage at a ten count after the curtain. Victor wants to see it with a blue gel this time."

"I thought we were using the rose gel, Hal," a short bald man in overalls shouted back from a place nearer the stage.

"Naw, Victor decided he doesn't like the way that color looks with Natasha's dress," the man named Hal answered. "I know, it's a pain when these guys change things at the final dress rehearsal."

"Dress rehearsal," Charlie whispered excitedly, clutching Lindsey's arm. "This is so exciting! What's a gel?"

Lindsey shrugged. "It sounds like it has something to do with the color of the light on stage. Listen, we'd better find Emma and get out of here before we're thrown out."

They moved along the wall, trying to be quiet and remain unnoticed. They saw the dancers they'd followed in, plus five more, now dressed in their ballet costumes. The women all had their hair pulled back in tight buns and wore identical blue gauze skirts that covered their thighs. Their thin-strapped blue tops were beautifully decorated with silver beads. The men wore military jackets like that of the dancer on the sign, but theirs were blue instead of red, and their tights were green. The dancers spoke to one another occasionally, but mostly they warmed up at a free-standing barre that had been set up away from the stage.

"Look, they're doing pliés, like we do in class," Lindsey said, pointing at three of the dancers at the barre.

"And that guy is doing an arabesque on half-pointe," said Charlie, indicating a tall, thin black man who stood near the barre, balanced elegantly on the ball of one foot, while his other leg stretched out behind him at almost a right angle. "I guess we *are* learning stuff, after all," she added, pleased to be able to name the steps.

Lindsey nudged Charlie and pointed ahead of her. There stood Emma, gazing around as if she belonged backstage. "Figures she'd find her way back here," said Lindsey.

"*Pssst,* Emma, over here," Charlie called in a loud whisper.

Emma's eyes grew wide when she saw Charlie and Lindsey. She hurried over to where they stood. "What are you doing here?" she asked, her hands on her hips.

"Us?" Lindsey replied in an outraged whisper. "We came to get *you.*"

"How did you get in?" Emma demanded.

"The stage door," Charlie told her.

A small smile broke Emma's stern expression. "You guys sure have learned a lot from me," she said admiringly.

Emma's remark made Charlie and Lindsey smile, too. They knew it was true. Before they'd met Emma, both of them would have been too timid to ever sneak into a theater. Emma brought out the adventuresome side of their personalities.

"Isn't this a great place?" Emma asked enthusiastically.

"Are you okay, Emma?" asked Lindsey. "We came because we thought . . . I don't know, that maybe you weren't okay."

Emma's face didn't betray any emotion. "I'm perfectly fine," she said. "I just decided I wanted to see the opera house."

"Okay, I guess we were wrong," Lindsey said, still not quite believing Emma's cool pose.

Emma's eyes suddenly went round with alarm. "Uh-oh," she whispered. "I think we've been spotted." Charlie and Lindsey turned to see the man in the plaid shirt coming toward them.

"Who let you kids in here?" he shouted.

Lindsey and Charlie turned to Emma, wondering if she would be able to come up with a quick story. But Emma had drawn a blank. Instead of answering, she turned and ran toward one of the long velvet curtains that hung in rows along the stage. Panicked, Charlie and Lindsey bolted in the same direction.

"Come back here, you kids!" the man yelled.

How were they ever going to explain this to Miss Claudine? Or to their parents? They knew one thing—they were in big trouble now. The man in the plaid shirt was bound to catch them.

Charlie, Emma, and Lindsey realized they had no place to go but right onto the stage. There was nowhere to hide.

"Stop right now!" the man ordered in an angry voice. He was right behind them!

The girls turned around and faced him. Then they looked at one another. There was no sense running. They were trapped.

Then, suddenly, they heard a snap, and all the lights went off. They were surrounded by inky blackness.

Chapter Seven

Emma stretched out her arms and groped her way in the darkness. A velvet softness caressed her cheek, and she knew she'd walked into one of the long red curtains in the wings of the stage. Without a second thought, she stepped into the curtains and pulled them around her. It was the perfect hiding place!

She stood there, trying to quiet her rapid breathing. The theater was now completely silent. Then she heard the soft, sad strain of violins beginning to play. Soon a piano joined the violins, making the music sound fuller. There was a swooshing sound as the front curtains were drawn apart. A gentle blue light filtered through the heavy curtains Emma had wrapped around herself.

Cautiously, Emma peeked out from behind the curtains. The man who'd been chasing them was gone.

The stage was on her right. Emma was instantly mesmerized by the sight she saw there. In the center of the stage, circled in a halo of blue light, stood a ballerina, poised gracefully on the tips of her toe shoes. She held her arms in a circle in front of her chest and moved in tiny, quivering steps, seeming to vibrate with the chords of the violins.

The glistening gauze of her knee-length skirt reflected the blue light, as did the intricate beading of her top. Silver sparkles shimmered in her upswept hair. She seemed to Emma like some unearthly fairy queen, radiating light in every direction.

As Emma's eyes adjusted to the soft light, she noticed two more faces nearby. Across the stage from her, Lindsey and Charlie were also peeking out from behind the curtains. They'd obviously had the same idea, and wrapped themselves up to hide from the man in the plaid shirt.

They spotted one another at the same time. The girls smiled and waved to one another. The urge to burst into giggles was stemmed by the sadness of the music and the beauty of the ballerina in the center of the stage.

All three girls had fallen under the ballerina's spell. They moved quietly from their hiding spots to sit beside one another on the floor just offstage, unable to take their eyes from her.

The music suddenly grew more lively, several flutes giving it a new sparkle. A very handsome man strode confidently across the stage toward the ballerina. He wore a red military jacket and red tights. At the sight of him, the ballerina kicked up her heels with a small flutter. She leaped toward him joyfully, springing off the floor and into a grand jeté with the power and grace of a gazelle.

"I've seen them before," Emma whispered with a small gasp.

"In the picture," Charlie whispered back, equally excited.

"They're the two on the sign out front. You're right," Lindsey murmured, her eyes still riveted to the stage where the couple was now doing something she recognized as a fish dive. The man held the woman by her waist and dipped forward with the ballerina in his arms as she lifted both legs elegantly off the ground.

"No, that's not where I've seen them," Emma disagreed. "It was somewhere else." She pondered as she watched the dancers swirl around one another, their arms mingling near their bodies. Next, the man swept the ballerina over his head as if she were weightless.

The ballerina never shook or fumbled to keep her balance. She simply stretched her long arms in a circle over her head and bent her legs back in a pose so graceful that even her long, tapered fingers seemed perfectly placed.

"I've got it!" Emma whispered. "I read about them in *People Talk* magazine. Her name is Natasha something-or-other, and his name is Ivan something. They're both Russian. They trained at the Bolshoi Ballet School. They were in love, but she defected to the West one time while dancing in Paris. Then two years later he defected while he was in Toronto. It took them another year to get into the same company, but they just got married last summer. It's so romantic," she sighed.

"They really look like they're in love," Lindsey added.

The girls studied the ballerina's face. She gazed tenderly at her husband as she twirled around him. He looked back at her as if he'd never seen anyone more beautiful—as if she were the only person in the world.

Suddenly the music took on a dramatic, vibrant tone. The ballerina ran off toward the far corner of the stage and struck a pose, looking out into the theater as if she were trying to see something in the distance. The stage lights came up to a bright blue, and the man stepped forward boldly. He spun twice, then flew into the air in a series of jumps Miss Claudine had once told them were called barrel turns. He circled the stage with breathtaking speed. "It's as if he's flying," Charlie breathed.

No sooner had the man come out of his final leap and landed in an arabesque, than the sound of a muted horn rose up from the orchestra. From the stunned and sorrowful movements of both dancers, the girls somehow knew that the horn was calling the man away, perhaps to a battle in some war.

The couple ran toward one another and danced together very closely. He supported the ballerina gently as she spun in position in front of him. When she stopped, he wrapped a strong arm around her waist and bent one knee. The ballerina lifted her arms over her head, letting herself fall sadly to his left side. Then, once they were standing again, the man let go of the ballerina. The horn sounded once more and, with his arms still extended longingly toward his love, he backed away from her, moving diagonally across the stage.

The ballerina stood on her toes facing the man, her arms also outstretched. When he was gone, the lights dimmed and the ballerina was all alone in the blue spotlight, just as she'd started. She bent her head sorrowfully and began a very slow, very sad solo dance.

Emma watched the ballerina and felt tears welling in her eyes. She sensed the woman's sadness as if it were her own. The woman was lonely; the man she loved was gone, and he might not come back to her.

A hot tear rolled down Emma's cheek. Her story wasn't the same, but the feeling was. Emma felt abandoned by two people she adored and admired. Her father hadn't even bothered to pick out a birthday present for her. And neither had Kerry. She'd just bought some dopey book that her stupid boyfriend had recommended, never thinking about whether Emma would enjoy it or not.

But it wasn't the presents, it was what they meant, the care and the love that they should have expressed. Emma felt like she had lost a father and a sister all in one day.

An awful feeling made Emma's chest heave with a small sob. She felt all alone, as if she were invisible and there was no one in the world who could see her. Completely and terrifyingly alone.

Then she felt a warm hand on the back of her neck. She turned and saw that it was Charlie, and that Charlie had tears in her eyes, too. "What's the matter?" Emma whispered.

"I don't like to see you cry," Charlie whispered back.

Emma smiled through her tears, but it just made her cry all the more. Lindsey slid up next to her and put her squarish hand on Emma's knee. "It'll be okay, Emma," she whispered.

Emma put her arm around Charlie's waist and squeezed Lindsey's wrist with her other hand. Silently the girls sat that way, watching the ballerina as she swirled slowly to the floor and ended her dance.

Chapter Eight

Just as suddenly as it had gone dark, the stage was once again illuminated with bright overhead lights. The ballerina rose slowly to her feet, squinting her eyes and still looking dazed, as if she hadn't quite made her way back from the faraway world of her dance. Her partner walked back out and stood beside her.

From out in the audience, Emma, Lindsey, and Charlie heard the sound of a single person applauding. "Bravo! Bravo!" the man cried as he clapped. "That was brilliant."

"The *pressage* does not feel right, still," the ballerina said with a heavy Russian accent, a worried expression on her face. "I don't feel steady in the lift."

"Natasha, it was wonderful," the man said firmly. "*I'm* the choreographer, trust me!"

"It *is* her, the one in the magazine," Emma said to Charlie and Lindsey. She rubbed her damp eyes, brushing the last tears from her lashes. "That was so beautiful."

"And it was so—" Lindsey cut herself short, realizing that the man with the plaid shirt was coming up behind them. "Time to go," she said quickly, pointing him out to her friends.

Emma and Charlie looked over their shoulders and saw the man approaching. They were instantly on their feet, searching for an escape route.

"Stay right there, you kids!" he shouted at them. "I'm taking you down to security."

That was all the girls needed to hear. They turned on their heels and ran in the only direction they could—out onto the main stage.

The ballerina jumped back in surprise. "You were great!" Charlie shouted as she raced by the startled dancer.

Equally bewildered, her partner stepped forward to see what was going on, blocking the path of the man in the plaid shirt. The two men tried to get out of each other's way, first moving together to the right, then to the left in an awkward little dance. Finally, each took a breath and moved to the opposite side.

This confusion gave Emma, Lindsey, and Charlie just enough time to scamper down the side stage steps and out into the theater. Still the man was right behind them. "Now I'm angry," he shouted as he chased them down the side aisle of the theater.

"Cut across," Lindsey yelled to the others. The girls separated, and each ran across the theater, squeezing through the narrow aisles of seats. The man's larger size made it harder for him to move through the aisles as easily.

They came to the wide center aisle leading from the stage to the door while the man was still struggling through a narrow row of seats. A quick look toward the stage showed them that the entire ballet cast was standing there watching. Some were laughing, others scowling. "Run for it, kids," one dancer yelled. "He's gaining on you."

"Get them, Hal," called another. "My money's on you."

Hal glared back at the stage and leaped over a row of seats. The girls charged toward the back of the theater.

"Go up! Up!" Emma shouted once they had crashed through the door and into the red-carpeted lobby. "He'll probably look for us by the front door."

The girls scrambled up the winding stairs leading to the second floor. The steps were close together and hard to run up, but they made it to the second landing. Ducking behind the railing of the upper balcony, they peered down. Emma had been right. The man was looking for them by the front door.

"Oh, no!" moaned Emma. "He's talking to the security guard." Charlie and Lindsey saw that the man was speaking angrily to the guard who'd let Emma in the front door. The guard was shaking his head and shrugging his shoulders.

"Uh-oh," Charlie gasped. "Our pal Hal is turning around and coming toward the back of the theater. I hope he doesn't come up here." They held their breath and crouched lower as the man stood craning his neck to study the upper floors of the theater. Finally he shook his head in disgust and headed back inside.

"Do you think the guard will just let us walk out?" Charlie asked.

"Or do you think he'll grab us and call our parents and get us into horrendous trouble?" added Lindsey gloomily.

"I have to think," said Emma. She closed her eyes and drew her brows together in an expression of fierce concentration. Charlie and Lindsey watched her, hopeful.

"Okay," Emma said, opening her eyes. "We have two choices. We can try to sneak back to the stage door where you two came in. . . ."

Lindsey and Charlie shook their heads. "No way," said Lindsey. "I'm not going back there."

"Then our only other choice is to take a chance and hope that the security guard is a nice guy," Emma said. "He did let me in."

The girls looked down at the security guard. He was settled behind his table once again, watching his small portable TV.

"He likes TV," said Charlie. "That's a good sign."

"It sounds like he might be watching a football game, too," Lindsey said. "I hear a lot of cheering. He'd probably rather see the end of that than be bothered with us."

"Makes sense," Emma agreed. "So, let's take our chances."

Slowly the girls got up and walked down the white staircase. "Nice chandelier," Charlie said, pointing up to the large, elaborate chandelier that hung like a giant star from the ceiling.

"It *is* a beautiful theater," Charlie said. "There sure isn't anything like it in Eastbridge."

"I told you," Emma said, smiling at Charlie. "There are a lot of nice things about Eastbridge, though," she added. Charlie and Lindsey smiled back at her. It felt good to be friends again.

When they came to the bottom floor, they looked at one another nervously. There was no sense trying to sneak past the guard, because they knew the front door was locked. They had no choice but to ask him to let them out.

The guard looked up and grew angry when he saw them. "You kids almost cost me my job!" His stern gaze fell on Lindsey and Charlie. "How did you two get in?"

"The stage door," Charlie answered politely.

The guard rolled his eyes. "You kids," he mumbled. "And I thought *you* were looking for your mother!" he scolded Emma. "I didn't expect you to be running around backstage."

Just then there was a roar from the TV set. The guard looked back at it. "Who's winning?" Lindsey asked.

"The Jets are now," he answered happily. "They just scored."

Lindsey and the guard stood together a minute, intently watching the game, while Emma and Charlie shifted nervously from foot to foot. "Run! Run!" Lindsey screamed excitedly at the TV.

"All right!" yelled the guard. "Way to go!"

A commercial came on and the guard looked up, remembering the problem at hand. "Okay, just get out of here," he said, taking the key ring from his belt. "I never saw you, okay?"

"Thanks a lot," Emma said as the three of them slipped past the guard and through the door into the cold, damp air of the plaza outside.

"You're welcome. Now go," he replied with a small smile.

Emma, Lindsey, and Charlie ducked their heads against the freezing wind that whipped in their faces. "Wow! Your nose is red already," Charlie told Lindsey.

"I know. Let's hurry up and get inside somewhere."

"I guess we should get over to the State Theater," Emma suggested. "I hope Miss Claudine hasn't realized we were gone."

"I think she has," Charlie said glumly. "Look."

Cutting across the plaza, his hands jammed into the pockets of his heavy blue wool jacket and his blond hair whipping in the wind, was Adrian. He'd spotted them, and he didn't look pleased.

"Where have you been?" he asked angrily. "Claudine is out of her mind with worry about you three."

Emma, Charlie, and Lindsey looked at one another and then back at Adrian. They really didn't have a good excuse—except that Emma had been having a really terrible time . . . and it was her birthday . . . and they hadn't meant to cause any trouble. But, it didn't seem like the right time to try to explain.

"Sorry," they murmured sheepishly, their heads down.

"You should be," Adrian told them. "I'm frozen stiff. I've been all over the place looking for you. I've been to every coffee shop, clothing store, and record store within five blocks of here. Where'd you go?"

"Um . . . we were in there," Lindsey answered, pointing toward the opera house.

"There?" Adrian yelled. "How did you get in . . . Oh, never mind. I'd better get you back before Claudine has a nervous breakdown. Come on!"

Not daring to say a word, they followed Adrian across the plaza. Large gray clouds hung in the sky above them, and dead leaves scraped the cement as they blew by.

The girls were worried about getting into trouble with their parents. But worse than that, the three of them realized, was the thought of Miss Claudine being angry with them. Miss Claudine was always so patient and understanding. They just hadn't stopped to think that she would be upset if they were missing—mostly because nothing ever seemed to upset her.

"Maybe she won't be mad," Charlie whispered to Lindsey.

"It does take a lot to get her mad," Lindsey agreed hopefully.

"She won't care," Emma whispered, yet her voice didn't sound confident. "Nothing bothers Miss Claudine," she added hesitantly.

Adrian led them through the glass doors into the State Theater. The first thing they saw was Miss Clau-

dine pacing in the lobby. She had rolled a *Nutcracker* program up in her hand and was twisting it nervously.

When Miss Claudine turned toward them, they noticed she was chewing on her lip, something they'd never seen her do. She caught sight of them and her tense expression relaxed into one of relief. "*Chéries,* you are safe!" she cried.

Just as quickly, her happy expression darkened and a thundercloud seemed to settle over her face. "Where have you girls been?" she asked in a low tone. "I am very, very angry at you. Very angry!"

Chapter Nine

"We're sorry, Miss Claudine," said Emma. "We didn't mean to worry you. It was really all my fault. Charlie and Lindsey just came after me because—"

Miss Claudine stopped Emma with an impatient wave of her hand. "You are back now, that's all I care about," she said. "Come along. The first act is about to begin," she added brusquely. "Have you got your tickets?" The girls fumbled in their pockets. Lindsey and Charlie pulled out their tickets and showed them to Miss Claudine. "Give them to the ticket taker and wait on the other side," she told them.

"M-Miss Claudine," Emma stammered in a timid voice. "I can't find my ticket."

Miss Claudine shut her eyes for a moment, as if to regain her patience. "Look in your purse," she instructed.

"I already did, but I'll check again," said Emma, rummaging through her large tapestry bag. She pulled out everything inside, passing handfuls of costume jewelry, makeup, pencils, and papers to Lindsey. "It's not here. I must have dropped it," she said at last.

Their teacher took a deep breath and then turned to the ticket taker. "One of my students has misplaced her ticket," she told the man. "I assure you it has been paid for. Could you please just let her through?"

The man remained stony faced. "I can't admit anyone without a ticket," he answered.

"Please, *monsieur,*" Miss Claudine implored sweetly.

Emma, Lindsey, and Charlie were convinced that no one could resist Miss Claudine's charm, but the ticket taker remained unmoved. "No one is admitted without a ticket," he insisted.

"Then I suppose we will have to buy another," said Miss Claudine, turning and heading toward the ticket window.

"I'm afraid you can't," said the man. "This performance is all sold out. I'm very sorry, but rules are rules."

"Oh, *monsieur,* have a heart. Where is your Christmas spirit?" Miss Claudine cajoled the man. "She is but a child. Children often misplace things."

"I'm sorry," the man answered.

"Listen," Adrian spoke up, sounding annoyed, "the ticket is paid for. I don't see what harm it would do if—"

"Never mind, *chéri,*" Miss Claudine told him, placing a calming hand on his arm. "There is nothing to be done. Would you please hurry and take Charlie and Lindsey in? Perhaps you will be able to get into your seats before the curtain goes up."

"I'm really sorry, Miss Claudine," said Emma.

Miss Claudine studied her face. "Yes, I think you are."

"We'll wait here with you," offered Lindsey.

"No, you go ahead," Emma told them. "No sense in all of us missing it."

"I'll stay with her, Claudine," Adrian offered.

Miss Claudine smiled at him warmly. "No, no, you go. Maybe we will change at the second act. Tell me where you are located."

Charlie looked at her ticket. "I'm L-twelve."

"And I'm L-thirteen," said Lindsey.

"I sat you three together, so you would have been L-fourteen, Emma," said Miss Claudine. "What a shame." Charlie and Lindsey waved good-bye to Emma sadly as the ticket taker admitted them to the theater.

Emma stood demurely behind her teacher. She was comforted that at least Miss Claudine had tried to get her into the ballet and no longer seemed so angry.

Miss Claudine turned to Emma and bent down to pick a long brown hair from Emma's poncho. "When the coast is clear, you scoot," she whispered. "I'll be fine. And remember, L-fourteen."

Emma had no idea what Miss Claudine was talking about. But before she could ask, Miss Claudine took her arm and led her back out into the middle of the now-empty lobby. She took her program and fanned herself. "It is very warm in here," she said to the ticket taker.

Suddenly Miss Claudine dropped the program and put her hands to her forehead dramatically. "Everything is spinning, spinning," she said. She fell back several steps and leaned against the wall. Emma watched in horror as Miss Claudine stumbled away from the wall, and then crumpled to the ground. Immediately Emma knelt down to help her. She was joined by two ushers and the ticket taker who rushed down the hall. They crowded around Miss Claudine anxiously.

Emma suddenly remembered her teacher's words. She almost laughed out loud. While everyone was distracted with Miss Claudine, no one was minding the entrance. The coast was clear. It was time for her to scoot.

She ran up the stairs and around the curved halls of the theater, looking for the L section. She climbed more stairs until she finally found it. The halls were empty and she knew the act must be about to start. She cracked open one of the heavy doors and slipped inside quietly.

Emma leaned back against the door, panting. The overture was dying down and the thick red stage curtains were going up. The stage was beautiful, set up to look like a Victorian parlor, with the largest Christmas tree she had ever seen right in the middle of the stage. Emma was transported into another time and place as she watched the happy family exchange presents.

Emma stood through the whole first act. She was mesmerized as the Nutcracker, now turned into a handsome prince, dueled with giant mice in front of

the tree. She watched with wide eyes as he defeated them and then danced with his young love, a real girl named Clara. As if blown by a magical wind, the tall windows of the parlor were swept open. Holding hands, Clara and the Nutcracker Prince ran through them, off to a land of enchantment.

The house lights came up and the audience applauded. It was the end of the first act. Emma quickly spotted Charlie and Lindsey seated several rows down just off the aisle.

The door behind her opened and Emma turned. It was Miss Claudine. "Are you okay?" Emma asked.

Miss Claudine smiled. "What I did was not exactly correct, but *c'est la vie.* The ticket was paid for and I didn't want you to miss the ballet. But, Emma, this is our secret. All right? Not even Charlie and Lindsey are to know about it." Emma nodded. "How do you like the ballet so far?"

"It was wonderful," Emma said sincerely. "And thanks."

"You're welcome. Now go find your seat."

Emma ran down to the empty seat beside Lindsey. "How did you get in?" Lindsey asked happily. Emma was dying to tell them the whole story, but she remembered her promise. "The ticket taker finally gave me a break, thanks to Miss Claudine," she answered.

When the lights dimmed again, the girls were instantly entranced by the exciting music and colorful costumes of the second act.

During the final intermission, Miss Claudine brought the class up to the refreshment stand. They bought sodas and wandered over to a booth where

T-shirts and sweat shirts were being sold. "That's a neat one," Emma said, pointing to an oversized white T-shirt with the word *Nutcracker* across the front in fancy purple writing.

"It looks like something you'd wear, Emma," Charlie agreed.

"I like it, too," said Lindsey. "The difference is that I'd wear it to bed and Emma would wear it to school as a minidress."

"I would," Emma laughed.

They saw Miss Claudine signaling them to go back to their seats. "You go ahead," said Lindsey. "I want to get another candy bar."

"You'd better not be late," Emma warned.

"I won't be," Lindsey assured her. "I'll catch up with you."

Charlie and Emma walked down the stairs with the rest of the class. "Where is Mademoiselle Lindsey?" Miss Claudine asked, suddenly looking very serious.

"Here I am," came Lindsey's breathless voice, several paces behind them.

They filed into their seats and watched the third act—*The Waltz of the Flowers,* and the beautiful and dramatic *Dance of the Sugar Plum Fairy.*

When the curtain closed, everyone in the audience stood and applauded. The curtain opened again and the dancers came out and took their bows. Some people in the audience yelled, "Bravo!"

The applause died down and the house lights came up. Charlie reached for her coat and felt something in her pocket. It was Emma's gift. She pulled it out and smiled.

"Happy birthday," she said, handing Emma the package.

Emma's jaw dropped open. "You got me a present even though we were having a fight?"

Charlie shrugged her shoulders. "Open it."

Emma pulled the paper off. Inside was a black plastic case. She snapped it open. The case held ten small squares of eyeshadow. "You remembered I wanted this!" Emma cried, throwing her arms around Charlie. "The colors are great!"

"I got you something, too," Lindsey said, handing Emma her gift.

"Watercolor pens!" Emma gasped when she'd ripped off the paper. "*Twelve* of them! Thank you, Lindsey."

Lindsey, Emma, and Charlie wiggled into their coats. "And here's one last present from both Charlie and me," Lindsey said, grinning and winking at Charlie. She pulled something white out from under her coat. It was the *Nutcracker* T-shirt Emma had admired upstairs. "Happy birthday, but promise you won't really wear it to school as a dress."

"How about with my black stretch pants?" Emma asked, holding the long shirt up in front of her.

"That would be okay, I guess," said Charlie.

"Thanks, you guys," said Emma. "You really saved my birthday."

Charlie and Lindsey put their arms around her, "You can count on us," Charlie told her.

With their arms still around one another, the girls followed the class down the stairs. When they got to the lobby they saw through the plate glass that snow was swirling all around. It had already blanketed the ground.

"It's so pretty!" Emma murmured. "It's like one of those glass balls with the snow inside."

"You saw *Dance of the Snow Flakes* inside," said Miss Claudine, referring to one of the dances in the ballet in which a small chorus of dancers dressed in sparkling white dresses had created a human snowstorm. "Now you see the real thing."

Outside, the girls discovered that it felt much warmer. Miss Claudine packed a snowball and tossed it at Adrian. He threw one back, and soon the whole class was laughing and throwing snowballs at one another.

"So immature," Emma heard Danielle say, as the girl stood with folded arms. At that moment a ball of snow skidded off Danielle's rear end. She turned angrily, but then smiled when she saw it had been Miss Claudine who had thrown it. "Oops, sorry, Danielle." Miss Claudine laughed. "I was aiming for Adrian."

The snowball fight lasted a few more minutes before Miss Claudine called it to a halt. "That's enough now, class," she said. She smiled and brushed snow out of her hair. "Let's go."

The class made their way across the snowy plaza behind Miss Claudine. "Hey, Lindsey," said Emma shyly, adjusting her purple beret on her head. "You wouldn't still have room for me on your trip to the Adirondacks, would you?"

"What about your father—and Kerry?"

"I'll see them for a few days, but I think I'd have

more fun with you guys. I mean, if it's not too late and all."

"Your father won't mind," Charlie cried eagerly.

"I'm pretty sure he'll say yes," Lindsey agreed. "It would be great if you came."

"Hey, look, isn't that your book?" Charlie said, pointing to the book laying on the ground, the one Kerry had given her. "Want me to run and get it before it gets buried under the snow?"

"Naw," Emma told her. "It was kind of dumb. I have everything I want right here," she said, patting her pocketbook where she'd put their gifts.

"We're going to have a great time this vacation!" Lindsey shouted.

"A great, great time!" Emma yelled, kicking up a spray of snow in front of her. "Because I have great, great friends!"

The three girls held hands and continued across the plaza as the snow danced around them.